This book belongs to:

.............................................

Retold by Gaby Goldsack
Illustrated by Ruth Galloway

Language consultants: Betty Root and Monica Hughes

This edition published by Parragon in 2009

Parragon
Queen Street House
4 Queen Street
Bath BA1 1HE, UK

ISBN 978-1-4054-8705-4
Printed in China

# The Gingerbread Man

# PaRragon

Bath · New York · Singapore · Hong Kong · Cologne · Delhi · Melbourne

# Notes for Parents

These **Gold Stars**® reading books encourage and support children who are learning to read.

## Starting to read

• Start by reading the book aloud to your child. Take time to talk about the pictures. They often give clues about the story. The easy-to-read speech bubbles provide an excellent 'joining-in' activity.

• Over time, try to read the same book several times. Gradually your child will want to read the book aloud with you. It helps to run your finger under the words as you say them.

• Occasionally, stop and encourage your child to continue reading aloud without you. Join in again when your child needs help.

This is the next step towards helping your child become an independent reader.

• Finally, your child will be ready to read alone. Listen carefully and give plenty of praise. Remember to make reading an enjoyable experience.

## Using your stickers

The fun colour stickers in the centre of the book and fold-out scene board at the back will help your child re-enact parts of the story, again and again.

## Remember these four stages:

• Read the story **to** your child.

• Read the story **with** your child.

• Encourage your child to read **to you**.

• Listen to your child read **alone**.

Once upon a time there was a little old man and a little old woman.

One day the little old woman made a gingerbread man.

9

The little old woman put the gingerbread man in the oven to bake. The little old woman and the little old man waited.

Then the little old man opened the oven. Out jumped the gingerbread man.

Let me out!

Oh dear!

He ran off, singing,

"Run, run, as fast as you can,

You can't catch me,

I'm the gingerbread man."

The gingerbread man ran on until he
met a cow.

"Stop!" said the cow.
"I want to eat you."

Stop! I want
to eat you.

"I have run away from a little old man and a little old woman," laughed the gingerbread man. "And I can run away from you."

"Run, run, as fast as you can,
You can't catch me,
I'm the gingerbread man."

You can't catch me!

13

The gingerbread man ran on until he met a horse.

"Stop!" said the horse.
"I want to eat you."

"I have run away from a little old man, a little old woman and a cow," laughed the gingerbread man. "And I can run away from you."

"Run, run, as fast as you can,

You can't catch me,

  I'm the gingerbread man."

The gingerbread man ran on until he met a farmer.

"Stop!" said the farmer. "I want to eat you."

"I have run away from a little old man, a little old woman, a cow and a horse," laughed the gingerbread man. "And I can run away from you."

Come back!

He ran so fast that the farmer could not catch him.

"Run, run, as fast as you can,
You can't catch me,
I'm the gingerbread man."

Catch me if you can!

The gingerbread man ran on and on.

He was very pleased with his running.

"No one can catch me," he said.

I can run fast!

Then he met a sly old fox. "Come here!"
said the fox. "I want to talk to you."

"I have run away from a little old man, a little old woman, a cow, a horse and a farmer," laughed the gingerbread man. "And I can run away from you."

20

"Run, run,
as fast as you can,
You can't catch me,
I'm the gingerbread man."

The fox ran after the gingerbread man.
The gingerbread man ran faster still.

Soon they came to a river. "How will I cross
the river?" asked the gingerbread man.

"Jump on my tail. I will take you across," said the sly old fox.

The gingerbread man jumped onto the fox's tail.

The fox began to swim across the river.

# Splash!

Soon he said to the gingerbread man, "My tail is tired. Jump onto my back."

So the gingerbread man did.

Jump on my back!

Then the fox said, "My back is tired. Jump onto my nose."

So the gingerbread man did.

Soon they reached the other side.
The fox threw the gingerbread man
into the air.

Snap!

Then, gulp, he ate the gingerbread man
in a single bite.

The gingerbread man
never ran away again.

# Read and Say

How many of these words can you say?
The pictures will help you. Look back in
your book and see if you can find the
words in the story.

farmer

cow

gingerbread man

fox

horse

woman

man

oven

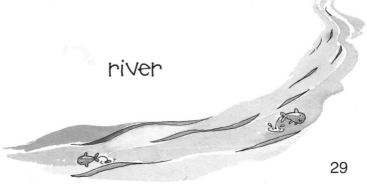

river

29

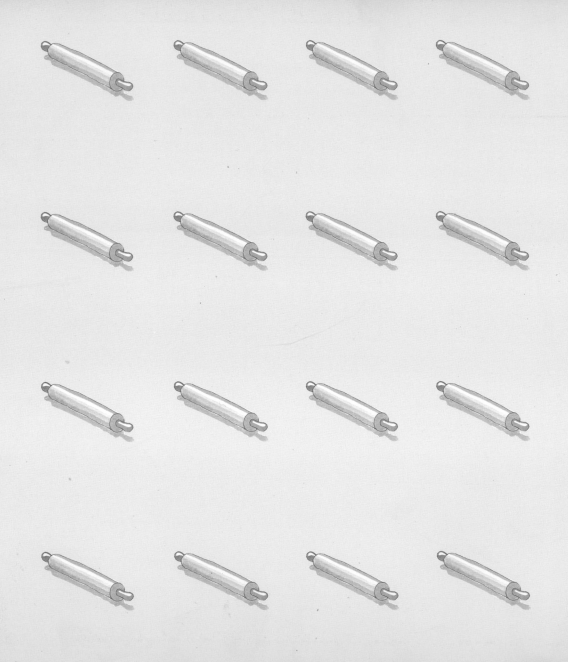